A Note to Parents and Caregivers:

With a focus on math, science, and social studies, *Read-it!* Readers support both the learning of content information and the extension of more complex reading skills. They encourage the development of problem-solving skills that help children expand their thinking.

 The PURPLE LEVEL presents basic topics and objects using high frequency words and simple language patterns.

 The RED LEVEL presents familiar topics using common words and repeating sentence patterns.

 The BLUE LEVEL presents new ideas using a larger vocabulary and varied sentence structure.

 The YELLOW LEVEL presents more challenging ideas, a broad vocabulary, and wide variety in sentence structure.

 The GREEN LEVEL presents more complex ideas, an extended vocabulary range, and expanded language structures.

 The ORANGE LEVEL presents a wide range of ideas and concepts using challenging vocabulary and complex language structures.

When sharing a content focused book with your child, read to find out facts and concepts, pausing often to restate and talk about the new information. The realistic story format provides an opportunity to talk about the language used, and to learn about reading to problem-solve for information. Encourage children to measure, make maps, and consider other situations that allow them to apply what they are learning.

There is no right or wrong way to share books with children. Find time to read and share new learning with your child, and pass on the legacy of literacy.

Adria F. Klein, Ph.D.
Professor Emeritus
California State University
San Bernardino, California

Editor: Shelly Lyons
Designer: Tracy Davies
Page Production: Melissa Kes
Art Director: Nathan Gassman
Associate Managing Editor: Christianne Jones
The illustrations in this book were created with acrylics.

Picture Window Books
5115 Excelsior Boulevard
Suite 232
Minneapolis, MN 55416
877-845-8392
www.picturewindowbooks.com

Printed in the United States of America.

All books published by Picture Window Books
are manufactured with paper containing at least
10 percent post-consumer waste.

Library of Congress Cataloging-in-Publication Data
Gunderson, Jessica.
Friends and flowers / by Jessica Gunderson ; illustrated by Cori Doerrfeld.
p. cm. — (Read-it! readers: Science)
ISBN-13: 978-1-4048-2291-7 (library binding)
ISBN-10: 1-4048-2291-7 (library binding)
1. Tulips—Juvenile literature. 2. Botany projects—Juvenile literature. I. Doerrfeld,
Cori, ill. II. Title.
QK495.L72G86 2008
584'.32—dc22   2007004563

Friends and Flowers

by Jessica Gunderson
illustrated by Cori Doerrfeld

Special thanks to our advisers for their expertise:

Mary Meyer, Ph.D.
Professor and Extension Horticulturist
University of Minnesota, Department of Horticultural Science
Minnesota Landscape Arboretum, Chaska, Minnesota

Adria F. Klein, Ph.D.
Professor Emeritus, California State University
San Bernardino, California

PICTURE WINDOW BOOKS
Minneapolis, Minnesota

Lindsey's best friend, Julia, lived next door. Julia's garden was Lindsey's favorite place in the whole world. It bloomed with every flower Lindsey could name. Lindsey loved the tulips the most. They blossomed each spring.

One day, Julia had bad news. "I'm moving away," Julia told Lindsey.

Lindsey wondered what she would do without her best friend. She couldn't imagine a day without Julia.

On a gray October day, Julia's family loaded the moving truck.

"I'm going to miss you," Lindsey said.

"I have a gift for you," Julia said. She held out a round bulb that looked like a small onion.

"What is it?" Lindsey asked.

"It's a tulip bulb," Julia said. "Plant it in your garden. Every year, you'll have a flower to remember me by."

Bulbs come in different sizes. Some are as small as a kidney bean. Others can weigh more than 10 pounds (4.5 kilograms).

"I'll remember our tea parties in the garden," Lindsey promised.

"Don't forget our lily hats," Julia said.
"Or our petunia necklaces," Lindsey added, laughing.

Tulips, daffodils, and some other flowers are called perennials. Perennials bloom year after year. The flowers produce seeds and then die after the growing season. But the bulbs remain alive beneath the soil. The next year, new flowers grow.

But when Julia was gone, Lindsey did not feel like laughing anymore.

"How will I ever find another friend like Julia?" Lindsey asked her mother.

"You won't find anyone exactly like Julia," Mom said. "But you will make new friends."

"When?" Lindsey asked.

Mom smiled and looked at the tulip bulb in Lindsey's hand. "By the time your tulip blooms, you will have a new friend," Mom said.

A flower bulb has everything the plant needs to grow. The beginnings of the stem, leaves, and buds are inside the bulb. It also holds a supply of food for the plant.

Lindsey wanted to keep the bulb beside her bed so she could remember Julia.

But her mother disagreed. "We have to plant it before winter," Mom said.

"Won't the bulb freeze when it snows?" Lindsey asked.

"No. The cold weather helps the flower bud grow," Mom explained. "But we must watch for rabbits and squirrels. They like to dig up bulbs to eat."

Lindsey chose a sunny corner of the garden to plant the bulb. She planted it near her mother's rosebushes.

Tulips need a lot of sun. Tulip bulbs also need to be planted on higher ground so water drains away from them. If the bulb sits too long in watery soil, it will rot.

11

Lindsey dug a hole in the soil. She used a ruler to make sure it was about six inches deep. She placed the bulb inside.

"Make sure the pointed end faces up," Mom said. "The roots grow from the other end."

1
2
3
4
5
6
7
8
9
10
11
12
13
14
15
16

One end of a bulb is usually thinner or more pointed than the other end. The pointed end needs to be planted facing upward. The round end contains the basal plate. The roots grow from the basal plate.

Lindsey patted the loose soil over the bulb. "Now, grow!" she said to the ground.

Mom laughed and said, "The tulip won't bloom until spring."

But spring was months away. Would it really take that long for the flower to bloom? Would it really take that long to make a new friend?

One day while she was raking leaves, Lindsey heard a strange noise. She stood still and listened. It wasn't the wind. The sound was coming from the garden.

Lindsey tiptoed toward the garden. She saw a little pink nose behind the rosebush. She saw a fuzzy body and a snowball-shaped tail. White ears pointed to the sky.

Lindsey's heart pounded. She had to do something. The rabbit would eat her tulip bulb.

Rabbits, squirrels, and other rodents like to eat plants from flower and vegetable gardens. Rabbits eat carrots and lettuce. Sometimes they also dig up bulbs from the ground.

"Go away!" Lindsey yelled. "Go eat a carrot. Stay away from my tulip!"

But the rabbit just looked at her. It did not hop away. It did not even move.

"Please don't eat my tulip," Lindsey begged.

Still, the rabbit did not move.

The rabbit hopped around the garden. Its pink nose wrinkled as it smelled the ground.

"Shoo!" cried Lindsey. She took a step toward it.

Finally, the rabbit jumped away. But Lindsey knew it would be back again.

"My tulip is in trouble," she cried.

That evening, Lindsey told her mother, "Rabbits are going to eat my tulip!"

"We can use a mix of hot-pepper sauce and water to keep them away," Mom said. "Because the mix is natural, it won't hurt animals."

Some gardeners cover their bulbs in hot-pepper sauce before planting them. The sauce is a safe way to keep rabbits, squirrels, and other rodents away from bulbs.

20

The next day, Lindsey and her mom sprayed
the hot-pepper sauce mix on the soil.

"How will this keep the rabbits away?"
Lindsey asked.

"Hot-pepper sauce is very spicy. Rabbits and
squirrels don't like the taste of it," Mom said.

Every day that winter, Lindsey checked
her tulip bulb. No rabbits bothered it. Lindsey
couldn't wait for her tulip to grow.

But the tulip was already growing. After Lindsey had planted the bulb, the tulip had started to grow. Under the ground, roots spread from the bulb. Once winter came, the bulb stopped growing and waited for spring.

In April, the sun warmed the ground. Grass peeked through the soil. The house next door was still empty, but tiny purple flowers dotted the garden. Lindsey remembered the good times she had shared with Julia.

"I still haven't found a friend like Julia," Lindsey told her mother.

"Be patient," Mom said. "Your tulip hasn't sprouted yet."

The next day, Lindsey walked to the garden. As she neared her tulip, she saw a thin, green sprout. Her tulip was growing!

For the next twelve days, Lindsey went outside daily to check on her plant. The sprout grew a bit taller each day.

On the twelfth day, Lindsey saw a small bud on the tip of the stem. Her tulip was about to bloom.

The next morning, Lindsey heard sounds coming from next door. She saw a big orange truck in the driveway. A new family was finally moving in.

A girl about her age stood in Julia's old yard. Lindsey waved. The girl waved back.

"Is that your flower?" the girl asked. She pointed to Lindsey's tulip.

27

Lindsey turned and saw that a red tulip had opened its petals wide.

The girl ran over to Lindsey's new red tulip. "That tulip is really amazing," she said. "I love flowers."

"I do, too," said Lindsey.

The two girls sat in the grass. Lindsey smiled. Her tulip had finally bloomed. And it seemed a new friendship was blooming, too.

Life Cycle of a Bulb

bulb planted

roots grow

day 1

day 30

Activity: Growing Bulbs Indoors

Items needed:
- one medium-sized pot
- potting mix
- a package of small stones or pebbles
- Three or four daffodil or tulip bulbs
- a spray bottle full of water
- a sunny spot

Directions:
1. Fill the bottom of the pot with the small stones or pebbles.
2. Add about 2 to 3 inches (5 to 8 centimeters) of potting mix.
3. Place the bulbs in the pot. Keep the pointed ends up. The bulbs should not touch.
4. Cover the bulbs with potting mix.
5. Water your potted bulbs. The potting mix should be damp, not muddy.
6. Place the pot in a sunny spot.
7. Using the spray bottle, spray the potting mix with water whenever it is dry.
8. Watch your plants grow.

Glossary
basal plate—the part of the bulb from which the roots grow
bloom—to have flowers
bud—a flower that hasn't opened yet
bulb—the onion-shaped underground plant part from which some plants grow
leaves—the flat, green parts of a plant that grow from the stem
petal—one of the colored outer parts of a flower
roots—the part of a plant that grows down into the ground and takes in water and minerals to feed the plant
soil—another word for dirt
sprout—a new or young plant growth
stem—the main part of a plant that supports the leaves and flowers

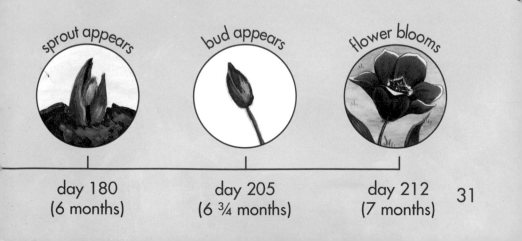

sprout appears

bud appears

flower blooms

day 180
(6 months)

day 205
(6 ¾ months)

day 212
(7 months)

31

To Learn More

At the Library

Bodach, Vijaya. *Flowers*. Mankato, Minn.: Pebble Books, 2007.
Corwin, Judith Hoffman. *Bright Yellow Flower*. New York:
    Scholastic, 2003.
Mitchell, Melanie. *Tulips*. Minneapolis: Lerner Publications, 2003.

On the Web

FactHound offers a safe, fun way to find Web sites related to this book.
All of the sites on FactHound have been researched by our staff.

1. Visit *www.facthound.com*
2. Type in this special code: 1404822917
3. Click on the FETCH IT button.

Your trusty FactHound will fetch the best sites for you!

Look for all of the books in the *Read-it!* Readers: Science series:

Friends and Flowers (life science: bulbs)
The Grass Patch Project (life science: grass)
The Sunflower Farmer (life science: sunflowers)
Surprising Beans (life science: beans)